IN EXTRA TIME

HANNAH COLE

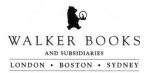

WALKER BOOKS
AND SUBSIDIARIES
LONDON • BOSTON • SYDNEY

For Patrick, Max and Eddie Neil

First published 2001 by Walker Books Ltd
87 Vauxhall Walk, London SE11 5HJ

4 6 8 10 9 7 5 3

This book has been typeset in New Baskerville

Printed and bound in Great Britain
by J. H. Haynes & Co. Ltd.

British Library Cataloguing in Publication Data:
a catalogue record for this book is
available from the British Library

ISBN 0-7445-5975-8

IN EXTRA TIME

Hannah Cole's first job was teaching adults
with learning difficulties. She now teaches
autistic children. She is the author of a
number of stories for young readers,
including *Our Horrible Friend*, *The Best Day
of the Week* and the popular football story
Kick-off. Hannah lives in Oxford with her
partner and their three children.

Books by the same author

Kick-off

The Best Day of the Week

Contents

Football
after School

"Football after school, Ibby?" Nick whispered. "I've got my ball."

"All right," Ibby whispered back. "I'll ask Brendan if he can play."

"Don't bother," said Nick. "He's useless."

"He's my friend," said Ibby. "And he likes playing."

Nick shrugged his shoulders. "Suit yourself."

Brendan was no good at football, but Ibby

liked him. So Ibby wanted to turn Brendan into a good footballer. Then it would be easier to be friends with him. He told him about matches that had been on the telly, and if they had a ball with them, he showed Brendan highlights from the game.

Now Ibby had decided that Brendan should stay after school to play in the playground. He wouldn't get better if he never played.

Ibby leant across the table and whispered to Brendan, "Football after school, Brendan?"

"I can't," Brendan whispered back. "I have to take my little brother home."

"Just ten minutes," urged Ibby. "He can play in the playground."

"Maybe five minutes," said Brendan. He wondered whether his mother would notice if they were five minutes late.

"Good," Ibby whispered. "Nick's got his ball."

"Don't you want to go home today, Ibby?" said Mrs Elgar. "I'm sure it's an interesting conversation that you're having, but the class is waiting... All right, after-school-club people can go. Green table can go. No, back you come, Sasha, and put your chair up properly. Blue table."

Ibby's table was kept till last. He and Brendan got to the door in five enormous steps each. Mrs Elgar couldn't accuse them of running in the classroom if they moved with straight legs.

"Go and get your brother," said Ibby. "I'll see you outside."

Ibby watched Brendan go down the passage to the little ones' cloakroom. He had to step over some lunch boxes and a small boy who was sitting on the floor, struggling with the laces on his trainers. Then he disappeared into a classroom.

Ibby ran out to the playground. Nick was already there, bouncing his ball.

"Brendan's coming in a minute," said Ibby. "Give me a header."

Nick threw the ball for Ibby to head, but he said, "We don't want Brendan. He's no good."

"I'm teaching him," said Ibby. "He'll get better."

Emma came running up. "Who's picking teams?" she asked.

"It's my ball," said Nick. "I'm picking for Man U."

"Bags me pick for Everton," said Emma.

Ibby knew that Nick would pick him, because he was one of the best players. He didn't have to wait around saying "Me! Me! Me!" So he ran over to Mr Batten's window and heaved himself up to the window sill. Yes, there was Brendan's brother Finn, standing at Mr Batten's desk with a large heap of coloured pencils. He was sharpening them. Brendan was over by the bookshelves.

Ibby banged on the window. "Come on, Brendan!"

"I'll be there in a minute!" Brendan called. "I've got to find him a reading book."

Ibby let himself down to the ground and ran back to the football game.

"You're on my side," said Nick.

They started to play.

Brendan heard the cheers as a goal was scored outside. "Finn," he said, picking up Finn's rucksack. "I've waited a long time for you while you sharpened all those pencils. Now you have to wait for me."

"Why?" said Finn. "Where? How long?"

"Five minutes," said Brendan. "In the playground. Because I say so." He led the way outside.

"I don't want to wait in the playground," said Finn.

"You can play with your friends," said Brendan. "Or you can read your book."

"Mr Batten says I need support to read my book," said Finn. "And those children aren't my friends."

"See you in five minutes," said Brendan. "Bye."

"You're too late," said Bimal. "We've got equal teams."

"We can change them," said Ibby. "Swap George for Tim, and give us Brendan, and then our team's got three feeble players, so it's fair."

Brendan didn't like being counted as

feeble, but he wanted to play. He didn't feel like a feeble player, but as no one passed the ball to him, he could not show that he was good. He dashed into a space and waved, and shouted, "Over here!" but the only time he touched the ball was when it went off and he ran to fetch it from the other side of the playground.

"That's more than five minutes," said Finn, who was walking along the lines painted on the tarmac.

Brendan kicked the ball back to the players. It flew high across the playground to the football pitch. He felt proud of that kick.

"One more minute," he told Finn, and ran back to join the game.

"Ibby! Ibby! Over here!" he shouted.

Ibby passed him the ball, but Sasha appeared from nowhere and kicked it away before he had time to touch it.

"Come on, Brendan," said Finn.

"I'd better go, Ibby," said Brendan.

Ibby did not hear him.

"It was boring waiting for you," said Finn.

"It was boring waiting for *you*," said Brendan.

"I was busy packing my things," said Finn. "You were just playing. Anyway, you're supposed to take me straight home after school."

"*You're* supposed to be ready to go straight home when school's finished."

Mum was cross that they were late. They weren't late enough for her to be really worried, but she had to be cross so they would know she meant them to come straight home.

"I had to wait while Brendan played

football with his friends," said Finn. "I had to hang about in the playground."

"Brendan," said Mum, "you should have come straight home. All right, Mary K. I'm coming."

Mary K had got fed up with being strapped in her special chair. It was meant to help her walk better.

"I only played for a few minutes," said Brendan. "I had to wait hours while Finn sharpened all his pencils and tidied his drawer. And he would have taken even longer if I hadn't found his lunch box for him and chosen a reading book."

"I know," said Mum. "You must hurry up, Finn. Here, Brendan, put Mary K's walker out in the passage, would you? But listen, I want you to come straight home once Finn is ready. Anyway, you're not allowed to play in the playground after school, unless you have a grown-up with you. It was in a school letter a few weeks ago. The teachers aren't on duty then, and they can't be responsible for you."

"That's stupid," said Brendan. "It's only like playing in the park. Teachers don't make rules about that. Anyway, there are always lots of spare mothers and things hanging about in the playground."

"The teachers don't want the worry of dealing with broken legs after school," said Mum. "I don't really blame them. And I can't expect other parents to keep an eye on you when I never take a turn. Go and get Mary K's shapes lorry, will you, Brendan? She can't put the shapes in, but she likes pushing it around."

"Nobody ever does break their legs," said Brendan.

"Anyway," said Mum. "Come straight home as soon as Finn's ready. All right?"

"All right," said Brendan gloomily, and kicked his school bag into the goal under Mary K's chair.

Football
at Lunchtime

"Never mind," said Ibby. "Even if you can't play after school, you can still play at lunchtime."

Ibby played football before school, and after school, and in every possible time between. If he wasn't playing, he was watching.

Brendan couldn't play before school because he and Finn were always nearly late.

He couldn't play after school. What about lunchtimes?

On Monday it was the infants' turn to have the football pitch. They liked it when Ibby refereed. Brendan didn't think he would learn very much from watching them.

On Tuesday it was the girls' turn. Brendan watched with Ibby, but he really wanted to be kicking the ball himself.

On Wednesday the big boys could play. Ibby always made sure that Brendan was allowed in the game. Some boys who were even feebler than him were never allowed to play. Brendan decided that when he was one of the best players in the school, he would let all the feeble players in. For now, he was glad to be allowed to play at all, even if no one ever passed him the ball.

On Thursday the boys were allowed to play,

but there was Recorder Club.

"Give up Recorder Club," Ibby said. "You can play the recorder at home."

Brendan went to tell Mrs Baker that he didn't want to be in Recorder Club any more.

"Why not, Brendan?" she asked, looking upset. "You're getting on so well, and we were going to start on the treble recorder after half-term."

"I need to play football in Thursday lunch break," said Brendan.

"Oh, is that all?" said Mrs Baker. "I thought there was a problem with the recorder. No, Brendan, I can't let you drop out. Recorder Club is playing for assembly next week, and then there's the old people's concert and we need you for the duet. Anyway, you're too good at it. I couldn't let someone as talented as you give up the recorder. It's not as though you play any other instrument, is it?"

"I could play the guitar instead," said Brendan hopefully. Guitar Club was on Mondays, when he couldn't play football anyway.

"Have you got a guitar?" asked Mrs Baker.

"Not yet," said Brendan.

"Come on, Brendan. Recorder Club is only one lunchtime, and you do enjoy it, don't you?"

Brendan wasn't sure that he enjoyed it as much as football. It was nice to be good at playing the recorder, and it was not nice to be feeble at football, but unless he practised he would never get any better.

"I do enjoy it," he said, "but…"

"Good," said Mrs Baker. "The more you stick at it, the more you'll enjoy it, I promise. I've just written out the parts for a new piece.

You'll like it."

So on Thursdays Brendan could not play football.

Fridays was Wildlife Club. Brendan had helped to dig out the school pond and line it with plastic and fetch water from Bayswater Brook. He had helped to make nesting boxes to nail on the fence behind the canteen, and every Friday he had checked the Mini Meadow and recorded the minibeasts he had found.

"You've dug the pond now," said Ibby. "It's past nesting time, and there are plenty of insects. The Wildlife Club doesn't need you any more, does it?"

"I'm sorry about that, Brendan," said Miss Tavener, when he told her that he would no longer be coming, "but there are other children waiting to join the club, so one of them will be pleased to take your place. Thanks for the hard work you've put in."

Brendan had forgotten that there was a limit on how many people could be in the Wildlife Club, because Miss Tavener didn't want the Mini Meadow trampled by too many feet, or the birds and insects frightened by crowds of children. He felt a little disappointed that she hadn't urged him to stay, but he was pleased that he would have another day to play football.

"I don't see why you can't play after school as well," said Ibby. He thought Brendan should get in more practice. He didn't seem to be improving very fast.

"I told you," said Brendan. "Mum wants us to come straight home as soon as Finn's ready."

"That gives you loads of time," said Ibby.

"Finn takes ages to get ready. You don't have to watch him pack his bag. Play with us until he comes out."

That afternoon Brendan had to wait for Finn to sort out all the reading books. Finn had noticed that some of them had been put on the wrong shelves, and some had been put in upside down or even back to front.

"Mr Batten will do that," said Brendan impatiently. "It's not your job."

"It's not Mr Batten's job either," said Finn. "Mr Batten says we should all help to keep the classroom tidy."

Ibby was right. Every day while Finn was slowly getting ready to go home, Brendan could be playing outside with the others instead of nagging his brother to be quick.

"Take as long as you like," he said. "I'll wait outside. Come and get me when you're ready to go home."

It worked. Left on his own, Finn took longer and longer each day to pack his bag and tidy up. Mr Batten did not hurry him. He was pleased to have the classroom left so neat, and Finn was no trouble. Brendan was careful to leave the game of football as soon as Finn called him.

"You're late again," said Mum. "You seem to get later every day. You haven't been playing football again, have you?"

"We set off as soon as Finn was ready," said Brendan truthfully.

"You'll have to be quicker, Finn," said Mum. "Brendan, you must hurry him along a bit."

So every afternoon Brendan tapped on the classroom window and called, "Don't be too long, Finn." It made no difference, and there was plenty of time for football.

The other players got used to Brendan turning up to play every afternoon. He was always the last person to be picked for a team, or nearly the last, but at least he did get picked, even when Ibby wasn't one of the captains.

Brendan thought that when he was one of the best players in the school, he would find a better way of choosing sides. It wasn't very nice to wait like a pig in a market while the farmers decided whether you were fat enough to buy. Especially if you were a rather skinny pig. You could choose something quite random instead, like people who had little brothers versus the rest, or people whose birthdays came in the first half of the year. The teams would probably turn out fair, just by chance.

Brendan made sure that he was useful. He was always the first to run for the ball when it went off. He was always the first to take off his jumper and throw it on the ground for a goalpost. Mum got angry because he came home so often without it, even on cold days, but he couldn't pick up the goalpost and walk off with it just because Finn was ready to go. Ibby always put the jumper somewhere safe when the game finished so that he could have it in the morning.

"No one ever passes to me, Ibby," Brendan said.

"Don't wait for them to pass it," said Ibby. "Go and get it. Tackle."

Brendan tried to tackle Nick and tripped him up. The other side got a penalty.

He tried to tackle Elizabeth, and Elizabeth carried on and knocked Brendan over. He got a horrible scrape all the way up one leg and one arm. He couldn't ask Mrs Olingo in the office to wash it and soothe it, because he wasn't supposed to be in the playground without a grown-up. He had to put up with it, and it was sore.

One day he tackled Marcus very successfully, but no one cheered him. He had forgotten that he and Marcus were on the same side.

Ibby sometimes passed to Brendan, but Brendan could never score because there was always someone else in the way.

"Don't try and keep the ball to yourself," said Ibby. "Look for someone to pass it to."

Brendan looked, and while he was looking someone came and took the ball off him.

"You have to be quicker," said Ibby.

It was very difficult.

"Don't worry," said Ibby. "You'll learn. Practice makes perfect." Ibby was used to encouraging the infants.

"But I don't get much practice," said Brendan.

The New Team

Ibby's older brother played for Diplow Rangers Under-Twelves.

"Diplow Rangers are starting up an under-eights side for next season," Ibby told Brendan. "Training on Wednesdays. Anyone can come along."

"Most of next season I won't be under eight," said Brendan. "I shall be actually eight in October."

"That's all right," said Ibby. "You only have to be under eight at the start of the season. Or maybe a month before, or something. Anyway, I'm sure you're the right age. Why don't you come along to training?"

"All right," said Brendan.

"Six o'clock at the rec," said Ibby. "Shin pads."

"Shin pads?"

"You're not allowed to play without shin pads. But we've got lots of old ones at home. I'll lend you some."

Today was Tuesday. Tomorrow was the day. Diplow Rangers Under-Eights. Brendan's new team.

"Will everyone who turns up be in the team?"

"Depends," said Ibby. "Depends who turns up. It will just be training to start with. Then, if it looks as if there's enough good players to make up a six-a-side, they'll fix up some friendlies. Friendly matches. Not part of a league."

"What about the people who aren't good players?"

"Don't worry," said Ibby. "Training's the main thing. Once you're training regularly, you'll get to be good. My brother wasn't in the team his first season, except sometimes as a sub, but he's one of their best players now."

It could happen to me, Brendan thought. This time next year I might be the best player in Diplow Rangers Under-Eights.

Then he remembered that the first thing was to get to be one of their players, never mind the best player. And the first thing before that was to get to training.

"Where did you say it was?"

"The rec," said Ibby. "Six o'clock Wednesdays."

"Where's the wreck?" Brendan asked his mother that evening.

"The wreck of what?" said Mum. "A shipwreck? Oh, Brendan, take that off Mary K. She'll swallow the wheels."

"I don't know what sort of wreck," said Brendan. He took the plastic aeroplane from Mary K and put it down quickly because it was wet from being chewed. "It's a wreck where football teams practise. How can they practise in a wreck?"

"Oh, you mean the rec!" said Mum. "The recreation ground. You know, the playing field behind the church, where the swings are."

Brendan felt foolish. "I forgot it was called the rec," he said. He was glad he hadn't asked Ibby to explain.

"We haven't been there for ages," said Mum. "We should go down sometime."

"Tomorrow," said Brendan, but Mum didn't hear him.

"Pass me a tissue, Brendan," said Mum. "Oh yuck, Mary K. Here, wipe your mouth. Good girl. Brendan, can you play with her while I get the tea, please?"

Some little sisters are fun to play with. You can teach them games, and sometimes they even have their own ideas. Mary K wasn't like that. She was hard work, but Brendan knew that if he wanted tea he would have to get her out of Mum's way.

"Come on, Mary K," he said. "Let's go and play in my room."

"Thanks, love," said Mum. "Why did you want to know about the rec?"

"I've got to be there at six tomorrow," said Brendan. "Football training. Come on, Mary K."

He opened the door for Mary K. She stayed sitting on the floor, but pulled herself along with her feet, with a lap full of pastry cutters and a cheese grater.

"Hang on a minute," said Mum. "What are you on about? You can't be anywhere at six tomorrow. Six in the morning, or six in the evening? Either way, it's out of the question."

"Of course six in the morning wouldn't be any good," said Brendan. "Six in the evening, and only for one hour. It's a new football team starting up, and anyone can go along to training."

"Anyone except you," said Mum. "Now please take Mary K upstairs and keep her out of the way for half an hour, and if she goes straight to bed after tea I'll give you a game of ping-pong on the kitchen table."

"Mum!" said Brendan. "I've got to go!"

"You haven't *got* to do anything," said Mum, "except take Mary K out of the kitchen right now, before all this food catches fire."

Finn came in. "Shall I read you my new book?"

"Not now, sweetie. We'll read it after tea. You can set the table for me. Have you washed your hands?"

"Why not, Mum?" Brendan asked.

"I'm not discussing it now," said Mum. Brendan thought that sounded hopeful. At least she had stopped saying no. He could explain why it was so important to join Diplow Rangers now, before they got full up with brilliant players and were no longer desperate enough to let in feeble players like him.

"Hey, Mary K, stop! Wait for me!"

Mary K was halfway up the stairs. Brendan raced up just in time to stop her trying to sit down on a step far too narrow for her big padded bottom.

Brendan kept Mary K out of the way in his bedroom. He hid his head in the wastepaper basket and popped out from under it. She loved that. She would have gone on laughing at that for ever, but Brendan got bored with it. Then he threw his quilt over her head, but she was scared and couldn't pull it off, so he got under it with her and sang "Tommy Thumb" to her. She couldn't do anything very clever with her fingers, but she liked it when he tried to make her thumb stick out for Tommy Thumb, and her fingers for Peter Pointer and the others. Then he took off her shoes and socks and tickled her feet.

Mum came to fetch them down for tea. She didn't think Brendan could get Mary K safely downstairs on his own. It was harder than going up.

"Good grief, Brendan! What have you been doing? Your bed's all over the place, and there's bits of paper everywhere."

Brendan looked round. He had thought he was being so good that Mum would change her mind about the football training.

"We were playing with the wastepaper basket," he said, collecting up the scraps. "I'll tidy it all up. She liked it."

"I dare say she did," said Mum in a tired voice. "Oh, Mary K, where are your socks?"

"It's all right, Mum," said Brendan. "I put them in her shoes so we wouldn't lose them."

"Yes," said Mum, "and where are the shoes?"

Brendan remembered that the shoes were in the wastepaper basket, under all the rubbish. He tipped it out, and then he tidied it up for the second time.

"I'll do them up, Mum," he said, trying to be helpful, but he couldn't get Mary K's foot to go into its shoe.

"She needs new shoes," he said.

"She needs to learn to push her feet into them," said Mum. "It's like dressing a pudding."

"She's not a pudding!" said Brendan fiercely. "Puddings can't laugh. Mary K's got the best laugh in the world."

"Of course she has," said Mum. "Come on down. Tea's ready."

Six O'Clock

At tea Mum wouldn't talk about football training. She said she didn't want arguments at the table.

"I'm not arguing," said Brendan. "I only want to explain."

"That can wait," said Mum. "I want to hear all the news from school."

So Finn told them about his science class experiment with wet and dry things, while

Mum spooned mashed food into Mary K. Brendan knew that Mum didn't want to hear about the new Diplow Rangers Under-Eights team, and he couldn't think of anything else, so Mum told them what Mary K had done at nursery, and what they had seen on the way home and how the buggy had nearly folded up with Mary K inside it. Mary K had a banana and wiped it over the table.

When tea was over, Brendan cleared the plates away. Mum didn't expect him to wipe the table because the bit round Mary K's place was too horrible for anyone except Mum to deal with.

"Can I tell you about the football now, Mum?" he asked.

"You said I could read you my book!" said Finn. "I've got another one about Amy the Alligator. I'll get it!"

"We'll talk about football when the little ones are in bed," said Mum. "But it's no, Brendan. You can't go on your own, and I can't take you. This is what life is like at six o'clock in the evening. It's always like this. We couldn't pack anything else in."

"I'll go and sort the washing," said Brendan hopefully.

"Thanks," said Mum. "That would be useful. But it's still no."

Brendan pulled the clean washing out of the airing cupboard and sorted it into piles. He put his clothes and Finn's away in their drawers, put Mum's in a pile on her bed, and took Mary K's to her room.

He thought about what Mum had said. She had said that he couldn't go on his own to the rec. She thought he was a baby. Didn't he take Finn to school and back every day? He was old enough to do that, just because it suited her. But when he wanted to do something that suited him, then Mum decided he wasn't old enough.

Brendan threw Mary K's clothes on the floor and went over to the window. Down in the garden he could see the little plastic football goal that he used to play with when he was Finn's age. Finn never played with it. Mary K sometimes pulled it over.

Perhaps he would just go to training anyway, even if Mum didn't want him to go. He imagined marching off down the road on his own, while Mum was busy with the little ones.

Of course, he would have to cross Watermill Road. They sometimes had to wait a long time to get across there, because it was so busy and there were no traffic lights.

"They should put a pedestrian crossing here," Mum always grumbled. "Hold onto the pushchair, Finn. Brendan, be ready to go when I say. Ready? No, blast that blue car. After the white one. No, there's a van coming the other way. Ready? Don't run, just walk fast. OK … now!"

When there was a gap in the traffic they would dash across. That made Brendan a bit nervous, but if Mum could pick a safe time to run across, he could too. He wouldn't have a pushchair, so it would be easier for him.

Then he remembered Tammock's Alley. So what? Those big boys weren't always there, and even if they were, they wouldn't do anything to him. Probably.

No, it was no good. Brendan knew that he couldn't really manage Watermill Road or Tammock's Alley. Maybe next year, when he was bigger, but not quite yet. Mum was right: she would have to go with him.

Or could he walk down with someone else? There must be other children coming from this direction. Ibby lived over the other side, but what about Tim, or Anwar? Tim's father had a great big black dog. Brendan was not keen to walk along with that dog. But they wouldn't go to training anyway. They weren't that keen on football. It would have to be Mum.

Why was Mum making such a fuss? What was life always like at six o'clock in the evening? It seemed all right. What were all these things that Mum thought she had to fit into the evening?

There was listening to Finn reading his story. Lots of children never read to their mothers at all. But Finn wouldn't stand for that. He always took a long time, too. He didn't just read his story and get it over with. A real author had visited Finn's class and showed the children how to find out when a book was first published, so now Finn always read the boring page at the front of a book before he would start on the story.

Finn looked at all the pictures before he began, in case they gave him clues about the story. Then he would look at them again after he had finished, in case he had missed anything. When he had read the book once slowly, he had to read it again so that it sounded like a proper story. Brendan could hear him downstairs now.

"Look, Mum, they've printed all those coloured pictures with only three sorts of ink. Isn't that clever?"

The real author had passed a magnifying

glass round the class, so that the children could see the little dots making up the pictures. Brendan wished the real author hadn't. He didn't want to see the little coloured dots in every book that Finn read.

Brendan had a good idea. He could offer to listen to Finn's story on Wednesday evening. That would save Mum some time. Then she wouldn't think that six o'clock was such a terribly busy moment. And he could play chess with Finn, which was the other thing that sometimes happened at bedtime. Brendan could easily do that, although it was very boring because Finn made up his own rules.

What else was going on at six o'clock? Tea was over. Of course, there was the washing-up waiting to be done. Brendan had often heard Mum complaining that the sink was always full of dirty dishes. But if he was rushing off to football training, he couldn't offer to wash up after tea. And it was no use offering to do it before tea, when the dishes hadn't got dirty yet. The sink would have to stay full of dirty dishes.

What about Mary K? What did she do at six o'clock? Mum started getting her ready for bed. It was a long business. Mary K had to do her exercises. She liked it when Brendan helped, but Mum said that he made it too much fun and stopped her concentrating.

While Mary K was in the bath, someone had to be in the bathroom with her, because if she slipped backwards she just stayed on her back. She couldn't sit up again. She would drown. If Finn got in with her, then Mum did not have to watch. Sometimes Brendan did, but there was not much room for the two of them.

Mary K did her speech exercises in the bath, because any noises that she made sounded better in the bathroom. Mary K liked splashing, and there was always a lot of mopping up to be done after her bath. After training, Brendan could help Mary K with her talking, and then he could mop up.

It was simple. Tea could be a bit earlier, just for once. Mary K could have her bath a bit late, just for once. Perhaps just for once she could be let off her exercises. It was hard on such a little girl to do so much work every single day. As well as being hard on everyone else helping her with her work.

Six o'clock didn't have to be such a terribly busy time.

Persuading

"All right, Brendan," Mum called from downstairs. "Come and talk to me while I'm ironing. Finn's in the bath with Mary K, so we've got five minutes."

I won't argue, thought Brendan. I'll be very helpful.

"Shall I bring these clean clothes down for you to iron?" he shouted down the stairs.

"Those ones are already ironed, thanks,"

Mum called back.

Brendan looked at the clothes that he had pulled out of the airing cupboard. He quickly tidied them and put them back in a neat pile.

"Right," said Mum when Brendan came down to the kitchen. "Tell me about this football training. I do want to hear about it, but that doesn't mean I'm going to say yes. I really don't see how we can manage it."

Brendan wanted to say straight away that it was simple: they could have tea early on Wednesdays, and he would listen to Finn's reading and maybe help with some housework, and Mary K could have her bath faster and later than usual, and everything would be fine. He wondered where to start.

"What is this new team?" Mum asked. She pulled one of Mary K's shirts over the ironing board and began to iron the back. Mary K got a rash if she wore anything except cotton, so a lot of her clothes had to be ironed. None of Brendan's clothes needed ironing. He wasn't fussy. That should count for something.

"Diplow Rangers Under-Eights," said Brendan. "Anyone can turn up for training. Ibby's going."

"But why do you want to play football at six in the evening?" said Mum. "Can't you play with your friends at school?"

"I can," said Brendan. "But not very much. And I want to get better at it. There'll be a coach to teach us how to play better. And you can't be in the team if you don't go to training."

Mum folded the shirt neatly and put it on the table.

"Six o'clock is impossible," she said. "Look,

supposing once a week Mary K and I walked down after school to meet you, and Mary K and Finn could play in the playground while you stayed for football with your friends? You'd be allowed to stay if I was there, wouldn't you?"

"I would," said Brendan. "It would be good, but it's not the same as going to proper training."

He thought that even if he stayed after school every day of the week, he wasn't likely to get much better at playing football. Ibby gave him good advice, but he never got to touch the ball. At training he would learn how to get into the middle of things, and tackle and pass and shoot and score.

"But there's Mary K," said Mum. "And Finn. And tea, and housework, and bedtime."

"Why can't I…" Brendan began, and then

stopped. He realized that his voice sounded high and whiny. He started again.

"I could help with Mary K and Finn and tea and housework," he said, in what he hoped was a calm, sensible voice. "I could listen to Finn reading, and blow bubbles with Mary K in the bath, and clean up."

"I can't fit anything else in," said Mum. "Really I can't."

Brendan heard the tiredness in her voice.

"There's Mary K's exercises," she said.

"Walking's good for her," said Brendan. "She can't walk on the way to the shops and things, because she keeps going off the pavement onto the road or into people's front gardens. But she could walk at the rec. She could walk round and round for miles. She'd like that. Wouldn't it do instead of exercises just for one day?"

"She'd probably walk straight onto the pitch and get knocked over," said Mum, but Brendan knew that the rec was so big it would be easy for Mary K to be steered away from wherever the football training was going on.

"What about Finn?" said Mum. "He wouldn't be keen on hanging about at the rec for a whole hour."

"There's the swings," said Brendan, although he knew that Finn had never been very interested in swings or slides. "But anyway, there's millions of things that I can't do because of Finn and Mary K. We can't go for proper long walks because they don't walk well enough, and we never go to McDonald's because Finn doesn't like the food and Mary K makes a mess, and we can't go to the cinema because they wouldn't understand the films, and…"

"All right," said Mum. "I know it's tough being the eldest. And I suppose Finn could put up with one hour a week at the rec. But then we'll get home late, and you all have to have a bath…"

"Just for once we could miss having a bath," Brendan said. He noticed that Mum was saying "we *will* get home late", not "we *would* get home late".

"Mary K can't ever miss her bath," said Mum. "All that pee and dribble. Then Finn needs a bath to get him in the mood for bed. And you'll be hot and sweaty and muddy if you've been playing football. You'll all need baths."

"We'll be quick," said Brendan. "I'll help with the others. I'll mop up after them. I'll promise Finn a game of chess in bed if he's really quick."

"I don't know if there'll be time for chess," said Mum, but Brendan knew that he had won. Mum finished ironing the last shirt and spread it out to fold.

"We'll try it," she said. "I don't know if we'll manage it more than once, Brendan. I'd like to be able to take you, really, but sometimes it feels as if I can only just keep up with all of you, and work, and the washing and everything. If Mary K slept at nights it might be easier. I'm always tired. But I don't want you to miss out on things."

Brendan didn't want to have to think about Mum being tired, and Mum having to get up in the night to see to Mary K, and Mum having to get her work done while Mary K was at nursery.

"I can go tomorrow?"

Mum stacked up the dishes ready to wash

up after Mary K and Finn were in bed. "All right," she said. "If you'll really help to sort things out, so we don't get too far behind with everything."

"Thanks, Mum," said Brendan. He gave her a hug. Maybe he could help to sort things out on other days besides Wednesdays, so that she would stop feeling tired. He imagined himself cooking and hoovering and washing floors for his grateful family. Then he remembered the Diplow Under-Eights team.

"Diplow Rangers! Here I come!" he yelled.

"Mu-um!" Finn shouted from upstairs. "Mary K's eating the soap!"

"Don't let her!" called Mum. "She'll be sick!" She dashed off up the stairs.

Brendan looked round for something helpful to do. He switched off the iron and took the ironed clothes up to the airing cupboard. He fetched a nappy for Mary K, and then he set out the chessboard. He only put out eight black pieces and eight white, to make it a short game, because Finn's games really were very boring. He practised the new recorder music while he waited for the others to get out of the bath and felt very pleased with himself.

Training

On Wednesday evening Ibby walked to training with his brother Tariq. Tariq played for the under-twelves. Ibby had often come with him to watch the training or kick a ball about with the other younger brothers and sisters, but it was exciting to be coming to proper training himself.

"There's your lot over there," said Tariq. "You've got Dave. He's Joel's dad, and I think

Joel's got a little brother about your age."

Dave was a tall man in a blue tracksuit, carrying a bunch of footballs in a net. There seemed to be a lot of under-eights standing round him. Suddenly Ibby felt nervous. He was one of the best footballers at school, but he could be one of the worst here. Then he remembered that Brendan was coming. I won't be quite the worst, he thought.

"Go on," said Tariq. "I'll meet you after training. Have fun."

He jogged over to the big pitch, and Ibby walked slowly over to join the under-eights. He couldn't see Brendan, but he knew a lot of the other children. Marcus and Sasha were there too, and Tim and Nick.

"Hi, Ibby!"

It would be all right, even if he wasn't one of the best. He wasn't really scared.

"Look over there!" someone said. "Isn't that Brendan? He's not coming to training, is he?"

"He's got his little brother with him."

Brendan was walking slowly towards them. Ibby guessed how shy he was feeling. "Hi, Brendan!" he shouted. "I've brought your shin pads!"

Finn reached them first. "We've come for football training," he said.

"You're too small for the under-eights," someone told him.

"I am under eight," said Finn. "Even if I was only two, I'd still be under eight. But it's Brendan who's really doing the training. Mum sent me to find out what time we can go home. That's my mum over there by the swings, with my sister."

Dave, the coach, was listening. "It'll be an hour," he told Finn. "Tell your mum we finish at seven. Right, lads. Jogging on the spot, and get those knees up *high*."

"Aren't you going to play football?" Finn asked Brendan.

"Go," muttered Brendan. "Tell Mum seven o'clock."

Ibby helped Brendan to put on the shin pads while the others jogged. Finn watched them for a minute and then set off back to the playground. He looked very small in the middle of the huge patch of grass.

"Right," said Dave, the man in the blue tracksuit. "Let's see how fit you lot are. Good at running, are you?"

A few bold people called out yes, but most stayed quiet, like Ibby and Brendan.

Ibby had thought that they would learn to tackle and dribble straight away, but he was glad that the first task was just easy running.

Anyone could do that. Brendan looked pleased too. Ibby wondered if he was a good runner.

"Twice round the pitch," said the man, "and no cutting corners."

Halfway round for the first time, Ibby realized that Brendan was not a good runner. He was already falling behind the others. When Tim and Sasha streaked ahead, Ibby wanted to race on and overtake them, but he looked at Brendan's face and felt sorry for him. He slowed down and jogged alongside him.

On the far side of the pitch was the playground. Finn was standing at the top of the climbing frame, watching them as they ran round. "Get those knees up *high!*" he shouted.

"You come and do it," Ibby shouted back.

Brendan couldn't have shouted anything. He had no spare breath.

Finn slithered down from the climbing frame and came out through the playground gate. He ran to catch up with Brendan and Ibby, then stopped. "Can I run with you?" he asked, looking at Brendan.

"Of course you can," said Ibby. "Let's see how fast you can go."

"We couldn't fit Mary K into the baby swing," said Finn as he jogged beside them. "Mum said it must be ages since we came last, if she's grown all that much. I wanted to try her on the big swings, but Mum didn't think she'd hold on."

When they got back to where Dave was standing, most of the others were halfway round for the second time. Brendan slowed down, but Ibby urged him on. "Keep going.

You can do it."

"*I* can," said Finn. "And I've got my knees up high." He ran with his knees coming up so high that he tottered and nearly crashed into one of the other runners. Brendan was running as though his feet were heavy and it was all he could do to slide them along the ground.

They passed the playground again, and Finn went back to join Mum and Mary K.

"Come on, Brendan," said Ibby. "The others are there already."

"You go on," Brendan panted. "Don't wait." But Ibby grabbed him by the elbow and dragged him along until they reached the others.

Dave was asking the children their names and what schools they went to. There were a lot from St Katherine's, which was nearer to the rec than Brendan and Ibby's school.

"St Katherine's," said Dave. "We've always had good players from there. Your brother scored a few last season, didn't he, Josh? And you in the Leeds shirt – I've forgotten your name."

"Laura."

"Your brother's one of our strongest defenders."

Dave recognized Tim and Elizabeth and Marcus, because they had big brothers who played for Diplow. He recognized Ibby. "You're Tariq's brother, aren't you?"

Dave had met Sasha and Bimal and some of the others on a football course at half-term, and there was a boy called Nathan that Dave seemed to know well, because he didn't ask him any questions.

Dave seemed to be noticing everyone

except Brendan. Ibby thought he should push Brendan forward and make Dave see him, but Brendan seemed happy to lurk at the back without being noticed.

"So, it looks as though we're off to a good start. Right, anybody else? Oh yes, I don't know you, do I?"

"Brendan."

"Brendan, right. Played much football?"

"Not much."

"So long as you're keen, that's what we need. Right, let's get started."

Dribbling

"All right, let's get you in two groups. Stand in a line."

Brendan stood close to Ibby, but Dave chose the teams by pointing to everyone in turn and saying "green, yellow, green, yellow" so that no one was in the same team as the person next to them. Ibby was green and Brendan was yellow. Dave gave them coloured bibs to put on.

"Come on you yellows!" some of the children shouted.

"We're not playing a game yet," said Dave. "Training first. Where are the dads? Hey, Mike! Come over here and take one of the groups, will you?"

Greens went over with Mike, who was someone's father. Brendan went with Dave. He felt nervous. Perhaps he would be bad at everything to do with football. He couldn't even run as well as the others.

"OK," said Dave. "In a line. First man dribbles the ball to the line over there, and kicks it back to the second. Second man does the same. Off you go."

Brendan got in line and watched the others. It was easy. You just ran along and the ball went along in front of you. The line was a long way off, and some of the children needed two kicks to get the ball back to the next person, but Brendan was sure he could get it that far with just one kick. Perhaps there was something that he could do better than the others.

It came to Brendan's turn. The ball reached him rather slowly, because the last person's kick had been only just strong enough. He set off to dribble it to the line. With his first kick he found that the ball was different from any ball he had ever kicked before. It was heavy. It must be a real ball, a leather one. At school they only played with plastic footballs, but it was better to play with a real ball. It didn't float away as you touched it, like the plastic ones. It was solid, and seemed to notice what your foot was doing to it.

The only problem was that Brendan's foot didn't know what it should be doing to the ball. First the ball went off to one side. He ran and kicked it back on course. It went to the other side. He didn't seem to be going in a neat straight line as the others had done.

Sometimes he kicked the ball too hard, which wasn't really dribbling but saved time. Sometimes he hardly kicked it at all, and nearly tripped over it. It took a long time to get to the white line. Relieved, he turned and booted the ball back to the little far-off crowd. He didn't stop to watch it, but jogged back to join them.

"Somebody go and fetch the ball," Dave was saying.

Had he kicked it in the wrong direction? Brendan looked round. No, the ball had gone in the right direction, but much too far.

He went over to Emma. "Why didn't someone stop it?" he asked.

"How could we?" said Emma. "It was way over our heads. It was quite a kick."

She looked impressed. Brendan wished he had kicked the ball to the right place, but it was good he had managed to kick it so far.

"Dad," Nathan called out, when everyone had had their turn at dribbling. That explained why Dave seemed to know him so well. "Can we do some heading?"

"Maybe later," said Dave. "Right now we're practising passing. It's the most important thing in football. No good getting the ball if you just hang on to it."

He made them stand in a huge circle. Then Tim had to kick the ball to each person in turn without turning, so that he kicked to the right, straight ahead and to the left. They passed the ball back to him each time.

"Good lad," said Dave. "Did you see how he

used different parts of his foot? When you were dribbling the ball just now, some of you were trying to use the inside of your foot all the time. Then you tripped over the ball. We need to practise using different kicks. Right, Brian next."

No one moved.

Dave looked at Brendan.

"That's Brendan," said Tim.

"Sorry, Brendan. None of your giant boots, now. Hard enough, but not too hard."

Brendan's first kick didn't go far enough, and Dave said he'd turned his foot the wrong way. The next kick went in the wrong direction. He would have to practise this at home. The next kick went to the right person, but then he must have stopped thinking hard enough, because the one after that went the wrong way and much too far.

Nathan had to run and fetch it. Brendan felt embarrassed. Everyone was having to wait because of his mistakes. It took a long time for him to kick the ball to everyone in the circle.

At last it was time for the match, and Dave called the other group over. There were real goals, much better than the jumpers at school. Not the big goals at each end of the full-size pitch that they had run round, but two small goals, only as tall as Brendan, which must have been put up specially for this practice. They were going to play across the big pitch instead of up and down it, so as not to have to run so far.

Brendan thought the match would be like the games at school, where he never got to touch the ball. But Dave said they were playing one-touch football. As soon as the ball came to you, you had to kick it to someone else. It gave Brendan a chance.

When one of the green team forgot about the one-touch rule and kicked the ball more than once, Dave blew his whistle and gave the ball to the yellows. Sometimes it was Brendan who got the ball. He didn't know who he should pass it to, but at least he got to kick it. Sometimes one of the yellows passed the ball to Brendan because he was in the right place. Sometimes he managed to pass it to another of the yellows. It felt like proper football.

Then Dave blew his whistle and told them that training was over.

"Take your bibs off, and put them in the bag. See you next week."

Helping

"That wasn't a whole hour, was it?" Brendan asked Ibby.

Ibby looked at his watch. "More than an hour," he said. "My mum will kill me. See you tomorrow!"

"Bye!" Brendan shouted after him. Then he remembered his own family and ran to join them in the playground.

"I passed the ball loads of times," he called

out to Mum. "And I kicked it further than anyone. We ran all the way round the pitch, twice, but I'm not tired at all. We played one-touch football, and next time we might play a real game."

"That's great," said Mum, but she was not really listening. She was busy helping Mary K to sit down at the top of the baby slide. Finn was standing at the top of the ladder to make sure that Mary K sat down in the right place.

"Look at Mary K," Finn shouted. "We've taught her to go on the slide all by herself!"

"Nearly by herself," said Mum.

"I was on the yellow team," said Brendan. "We play with a real leather football. Do you think I could have one for my birthday?"

Then he noticed that they were waiting for him to be excited about Mary K on the slide. Quickly he switched off the footballer part of his mind and switched on the big-brother part. "Brilliant," he said. "How did you teach her, Finn?"

"Easy," said Finn. "We let her do it hundreds and hundreds of times. Every time I helped her a tiny bit less than the time before."

"She always wants to climb up," said Mum. "You know what she's like with stairs. Usually I just let her do it once or twice, and then I hold her while she slides down. But today we had plenty of time, so she's had lots of practice."

"At first I had to make her let go of the sides," said Finn, "and then push her down. But now, you watch!"

Mum went to the foot of the slide, and Finn touched Mary K's hands gently to remind her about letting go.

"Off you go, Mary K!"

Mary K let go of the sides and launched herself down the slope. Mum caught her at the bottom.

"Fantastic!" said Brendan. He ran to hug Mary K. "Clever girl!"

"You should have seen her face the first time," said Mum. "She was just as excited as we were."

"She looked pretty excited this time," said Brendan. "You're so clever, Mary K!"

"Come on, Mary K, do it again," said Finn.

"One more time," said Mum. "Then we must go."

Brendan pushed Mary K's buggy all the way home. He was grateful to her for being so interesting in the playground. Mum and Finn didn't seem to have been bored at all while he played football.

"What shall we teach Mary K next week?" Finn asked when they were nearly home. "Do you think she could go on the big slide?"

"Definitely not," said Mum.

"You could try getting her to say 'up' before you let her climb up," Brendan suggested. "She can say something a bit like 'up', can't she?"

"That's an idea," said Mum.

"How about that, Mary K?" said Finn, getting in the way of the buggy wheels. "You'll be sliding and talking as well, next time."

It sounded as though there might be a next time.

Brendan was very careful to help with everything he could think of when they got home. He folded up the buggy without being asked and put it away. He raced upstairs to run the bath for Finn and Mary K. When he heard Finn say that he was hungry, he ran down again.

"I'll make him some toast, Mum. Would Mary K like some as well?"

"No, thanks," said Mum. "She'll have her bottle after her bath, and that'll do her."

"Cup of tea, Mum?" said Brendan.

"I'd love one," said Mum. "You haven't left the bath running, have you?"

Brendan ran upstairs again. The bath was only a bit too full. He let some of the water out.

"Do you want to read me your school book while Mum undresses Mary K?" he asked Finn when the toast was ready.

"No," said Finn. "I want to read to Mum."

"Not now, sweetie-pie," said Mum. "I must get Mary K into the bath."

"I'll undress her," said Brendan. "Come on,

Mary K. Upstairs. Up! Up! Say 'up'!"

So Mum and Finn sat on the sofa with Finn's reading book, and they took so long that Brendan got into the bath with Mary K. He washed her dribbly face and her muddy hands, and his own muddy knees, and then they played with a sponge, and he encouraged her to shout and to say 'Ber', which was her latest sound. He thought it would be good if his name was the first one that she learnt to say.

Then Brendan remembered that it was late, so he got out and dried himself, and ran for his pyjamas. He spread Mary K's towel out on the floor and heaved her out of the bath. She was very heavy, and she didn't know how to help. She just dangled in his arms, and she was very slippery. He sat her on the towel and dried her all over, especially between her toes, which Mum was very fussy about. He put her pyjama top on so that she wouldn't get cold, and laid her down on the mat ready for her nappy.

"Brilliant," said Mum, coming up with Mary K's bottle. "Both of you washed already! Right, Mary K, let's find you a nappy."

"Here you are, Mum," said Brendan. "And here's the cream for her knees. Shall I put it on?"

"Yes, please," said Mum. "It is lovely to have all this help."

Brendan longed to ask whether it was so lovely that he could go to football training every week, but he decided that he had better wait and see.

Football in
the Park

"Training was good, wasn't it?" Ibby said to
Brendan at school the next day. "I'm glad
your mum let you come."

"It was good," said Brendan, "but I wasn't.
I'll never be any good."

"You will," said Ibby. "You only need more
practice."

"What do you think I should practise?"

Ibby thought that Brendan should practise

everything: running, kicking, heading, turning, everything. But perhaps that would sound discouraging.

"You could practise dribbling, maybe, and shooting. I mark a goal on our garage door with chalk."

"It's difficult at home," said Brendan. "Our garden's rather small. Last time I broke some of the flowers. A real footballer could stop the ball going in the wrong place, but I can't get good at that without practising."

"You could practise at lunchtimes, couldn't you?" said Ibby. "When we aren't allowed on the pitch, you could practise running, and get a bit fitter."

Brendan thought about that. "I could run round the playground, couldn't I?"

"Time yourself by the office clock," Ibby suggested. "You can see it if you climb up and look in through the window. The more you practise, the faster you'll get. My dad times me running down the road and back."

"But I can't do that till next Monday," said Brendan. "It's recorders this afternoon. I suppose Finn and I could run home after school. And Mum will be pleased that we're earlier than usual."

Finn liked the idea of running, but he dropped his lunch box and it burst open. The crisp packet and the satsuma peel fell out on the pavement. Brendan had to pack it up again and carry it himself. Halfway home, Finn said his bag was too heavy to run with, so they ran the rest of the way home with Finn carrying nothing and Brendan weighed down by bags and boxes. He felt his legs getting stronger with every step.

"You could practise at the park," Ibby

suggested the next day. "Dribbling and all that."

"I'm not allowed to go on my own," said Brendan.

"I go with my brother sometimes," said Ibby. "You could come with us. We could go today after school."

"I haven't got a real ball," said Brendan.

"Tariq's got one," said Ibby. "Ask your mum when you get home, and give me a ring. If you are allowed, we can meet at the park."

Mum said that was all right. "Ask Ibby if he wants to come back for tea," she said. "We're just having fish fingers and oven chips. It'll be easy to do a few extra."

They met by the basketball net in the park. Tariq came with Ibby. He was very big, but he was friendly like Ibby. He had heard about Ibby's plan to make Brendan a good footballer and he didn't mind helping. He thought of things for them to practise, and he threw the ball for them to head.

"Keep your eyes on the ball," he told Brendan.

Brendan couldn't keep his eyes open. He tried to, but they shut every time.

"How can you hit it, if you can't see where it is?" said Tariq. "Keep looking at it until you've hit it."

Brendan watched the ball coming, but then at the last minute he shut his eyes and ducked his head. Tariq and Ibby laughed, but they didn't get cross with him.

"Try this," said Ibby.

He held the ball just a little way above Brendan's head.

"Jump up and hit it out of my hands," he said.

That was better. Brendan could do that.

"Now I'll throw it really gently," Ibby said. "The ball's not coming to hit you. It's you who's going to hit the ball."

Brendan jumped, and watched where to hit.

"Great header!" said Ibby.

It hadn't really been a great header. Brendan's head had only just touched the ball, but at least he'd kept his eyes open.

Tariq threw the ball for Ibby to head. They took turns. Then Tariq showed them a trick, bouncing the ball off his knee and his foot so that it never touched the ground.

"He can do that for hours," said Ibby. "Give us the ball, Tariq. Let's have a go."

He managed a few bounces before the ball fell to the ground.

"You try, Brendan."

Brendan tried. It was impossible, but he thought it was something he could try in the garden at home. A ball falling on the grass couldn't do much harm.

They played a match, Tariq against the other two. Tariq won, seven–four. Ibby scored the four, but Brendan did manage to kick the ball a few times, and the others always shouted "Good pass!" or "Well played!"

"Do you want to come to my house for tea?" Brendan asked. "My mum said you could if you wanted."

"I've got to get back and do my homework," Tariq said. "I can tell Mum you'll be late, if you want, Ibby."

"Am I allowed to walk back on my own, do you think?" Ibby asked.

"I'll come and meet you," said Tariq.

So Ibby came back to Brendan's house for

fish fingers and oven chips and sweetcorn and tomato ketchup, with chocolate yogurt for pudding. Finn told him about the map that his class had drawn at school that morning.

Mum spooned food into Mary K, and Mary K liked Ibby so much that she kept turning round to smile at him just when the mashed fish fingers were supposed to be going into her mouth. Brendan wished that Mum had fed Mary K earlier. Sometimes she did have her tea before everyone else.

"Mary K, can't you keep still?" said Mum, scooping food off her cheek. "Sorry, Ibby, I know she's a bit messy."

"That's all right," said Ibby. "Babies are like that."

Then he felt embarrassed, because Mary K wasn't a baby.

"This is the messiest house in the world," said Finn proudly. "And Mary K is the messiest person in it."

Mary K was pleased to hear her name. She banged the table and made all the plates chink.

"Was there any football on the telly last night?" Brendan asked Ibby.

"No," said Ibby.

"There was a rabbit on our telly last night," said Finn.

It was true. There was a china rabbit on top of their telly. It was always there. Brendan sighed.

After tea Brendan took Ibby upstairs. They played football with Brendan's pyjamas until Mum shouted at them to stop. Then Brendan showed Ibby the crane he had fixed up at the end of his bed.

"Why is your little sister called Mary K?" Ibby asked.

"She just is," said Brendan. "I could be Brendan K, but it doesn't sound right." He remembered that other people had asked about Mary K's name, but really it wasn't any more strange to stretch Mary out to Mary K than to cut Ibrahim short to Ibby. A name can be whatever you choose.

They played with the crane. It was better at dropping things than lifting them up.

"How old is Mary K?" asked Ibby.

"Four," said Brendan. He wondered if he should explain that although Mary K had been alive for four years, she wasn't exactly four in the same way that most other people were four.

"Four?" said Ibby. There were four-year-olds at school, learning to draw, and count, and stand in straight lines.

Brendan thought it was too complicated to explain, so instead he said, "Finn's five."

"Why does Mary K have to be fed like a baby?" Ibby asked.

"She just does," said Brendan. "But she is learning. She'll feed herself in the end. And run about and talk. I help her to learn sometimes."

Ibby couldn't think of anything else to ask about Mary K, so they dropped some more things from the crane. Then they took it apart and made a better gadget for dropping pillows on people when they came into the room. They tried it on Tariq when he came to fetch Ibby and it nearly worked.

"Thank you for the food," Ibby said to Brendan's mum.

"Thank you for playing football with me,"

Brendan said to Tariq.

"Thank you for eating six fish fingers," Finn said to Ibby. "Now Mum won't say I'm greedy when I want more than three."

"Finn!" said Mum. "Visitors are welcome to eat as much as they want. Ibby was hungry after all that football. Come again soon, Ibby."

Goal Kick

Brendan waited to see what Mum would say about next Wednesday's football training.

At the weekend he was very helpful. He went to the shop for bread and bananas and a newspaper, and he fetched the washing off the line when it started to rain. He washed up after Saturday's lunch, which was easy because they had only eaten things that didn't need cooking, like cheese and bread.

While Brendan washed up, Finn went into the garden to count ants for his teacher, and Mum took the newspaper into the living room.

Suddenly Brendan heard a crash. At first he thought, It's just Mary K wrecking something, as usual. Then he thought, Maybe I can get there quick and clear it up before Mum has to. He felt that such goodness would make football training pretty certain.

He ran into the front room, and it was just as well he did, because Mum was asleep on the sofa with the newspaper on her lap. She must be very tired to have slept through that crash, Brendan thought.

Luckily the crash had not been anything breaking, just a pot full of pens and pencils falling off a shelf because Mary K had got one of the long cushions off the end of the sofa and was waving it around. If Brendan hadn't come in when he did, a lot more things would soon have crashed to the floor.

Brendan took hold of the other end of the cushion, but that didn't work. Mary K thought he was playing a game and laughed. Then she realized that he was trying to take the cushion away from her and screamed.

"Don't," said Brendan. "You'll wake Mum. Here, have one of the little cushions."

He tossed the little cushion around a bit to make it look interesting. Mary K let go of the big cushion and reached for the little one spinning in front of her. While she poked at it, Brendan put back the sofa cushion and tidied up the pens.

"Let's go in the kitchen, Mary K," he said. "I'll get you some spoons and things to play with."

Mary K played happily while he dried the dishes. As he was putting away the last knife, Mum came bursting into the room.

"There she is! I thought she'd disappeared! I must have fallen asleep!"

"You did," said Brendan. "I brought her in here so I could keep an eye on her."

"Thanks," said Mum. "I feel better after that sleep. Now, I must hang that washing out again while the sun's shining, and then we'll go over and see Granny."

"Shall I do something else useful before we go?" Brendan offered.

"No," said Mum. "You've done your share for today. You've been a real help."

Later Brendan heard Mum tell Granny how helpful he had been.

"We've made an arrangement," Mum explained. "He helps me round the house a bit more than he used to, and I take him to his football training on Wednesdays."

"Every Wednesday?" Granny asked.

"Every Wednesday," said Mum.

So that was all right.

On the next Wednesday Dave said that the most important thing to learn in football was controlling the ball.

"Last week you said that passing the ball was the most important thing," said Nathan.

Brendan wouldn't have dared say it, but Dave was Nathan's own father, so Nathan dared.

"You won't get a chance to pass the ball if you can't control it first," said Dave, and he made them dribble the ball in and out of traffic cones.

Brendan practised at home the next day

with a tennis ball, in and out of flowerpots. He and Ibby practised in the playground. Tariq took them to the park and set them a course in and out of bushes and trees.

Dave warned them that they would have to get themselves proper football boots. At the moment, trainers were better than boots, he said, because the ground was so dry and hard, but they wouldn't do if there was rain. If it rained, trainers would slide all over the place.

"Who's got proper boots at home?" he asked.

Most of them had. Brendan's heart sank. Mum had used up all her Wednesday evening for his football. He couldn't expect her to use up all her money as well.

Dave saw Brendan's face. "What size are your feet, Norman?"

"One, I think," said Brendan. He knew that Dave meant him.

"We've got some old boots of Nathan's at home," said Dave. "He's got big feet. You could use them if you like, until you get yourself a pair."

The next week Dave said that winning the ball was the most important part of playing football. If you can't win the ball in the first place, you don't get a chance to control it, or pass, or anything. Brendan couldn't practise that on his own, but he practised with Ibby. One of them set off from the litter bin, dribbling the ball, and the other one tried to get the ball off him before he got to the conker tree. It was even better when Tariq played with them. They played pig in the middle. It was hard work and they all ended up panting and sweating.

"You're getting faster, Brendan," Tariq said.

"Am I?" said Brendan. He knew he was. He felt lighter. It wasn't such hard work any more for his legs to carry him about.

"He runs home from school every day," said Ibby.

"We should do that," said Tariq. "Only I have so much homework to carry."

"Weight training," said Ibby. "Even better."

The week after that, Dave said that the most important football skill was shooting, and Nathan gave up arguing. Dave said that all the control in the world is going to do you no good, if you can't put the ball away once you've got it.

Brendan hoped that he would never have to play in goal. Everyone was getting better and better at scoring goals, but nobody was showing them how to stop the ball going in.

In the game at the end of that session, Brendan didn't have to play in goal, but he did have to take the goal kicks. Dave said that Arjun, who was in goal for the green team, didn't have a strong enough kick. He told him to practise in the park. "Not at home," he said. "The neighbours won't want to keep digging your ball out of their flower bed."

The first time the greens were given a goal kick, Dave called out to Brendan, "You take it, Bradley. Just boot it as hard as you can."

It was only a training game, but Brendan felt nervous in case the ball went in the wrong direction, the way it had on that first Wednesday. But he was a better footballer now, and the ball went more or less where he aimed it. He booted it, and it flew nearly to the other end of the pitch. Of course, it was only a short pitch.

"Great kick, Brendan!" someone shouted. Brendan looked round. He was used to Ibby shouting encouraging things like that, but this time it was someone else. He really had kicked it well. While he stood feeling pleased with himself, one of his team had scored a goal, and that was because of his kick getting the ball up to the right place.

He was definitely getting better. He wasn't always the last person to be picked to play after school. At training Dave no longer had to say kind things to him. Sometimes he said that Brendan was doing well, and sometimes he said he was doing badly. Brendan was just one of the players. Maybe he would be picked for the first match, which was next Sunday morning, against Gadsmere Rangers. Not very likely, because it was only six-a-side and nearly everyone was better than him.

But there was a chance. Tim kept missing training, and Dave said you couldn't expect to be picked for the team if you didn't turn up for training. Emma had gone to Florida for a fortnight with her father. Daniel had stopped coming because he had decided to join the swimming club instead, and although Josh came to training, he was never going to be able to play in matches because he sang in his church choir on Sunday mornings.

Brendan thought that George didn't look very well. He kept coughing. If he could get a bit worse, and perhaps Arjun, who was a good friend of his, could catch the cough as well, that would improve Brendan's chances. Sometimes when Nathan was cheeky, Dave would tell him, "One more word out of you, and you're out of the squad!" but it wasn't likely that Nathan would be cheeky enough.

Brendan felt a bit mean, hoping that all these people would miss the game. They probably wanted to play just as much as he did. But he couldn't help feeling that his wanting was bigger than theirs.

The Match

There was no kit for Diplow's new under-
eights team. Dave hoped that next term they
would find a sponsor to pay for yellow shirts,
red shorts and white socks, like Diplow's
older teams. For now, they would have to
wear the leftovers from this year's under-tens,
who had just got a new kit.

The shirts were faded, and they were the
wrong size for most of the team. Ibby was

lucky. He was big enough to fit in his but the others were much too small. They put on the shirts and flapped their hands at each other, with the long sleeves dangling.

"Come on, roll them up," said Dave. "Look businesslike. And tuck the shirts into your shorts."

The shorts were short enough, but it would have been better if they had been longer, because the tucked-in shirts stuck out at the bottom, a yellow frill round the tops of their legs. The main problem with the shorts was that they were too big round the middle. Ten-year-olds have bigger tummies than seven-year-olds and except for Nick, who was quite fat, they had to clutch the tops of the shorts to stop them falling down.

"How can we play if we have to hold our shorts up?" said Nathan. "Dad, you should have put new elastic in them."

"I should have got you to put new elastic in them," said Dave. "But luckily I thought of bringing safety pins. Right, then, line up if you need a safety pin to hold your shorts up."

The socks looked funny because, when they pulled them up, the sock heel came way past the real foot heel, halfway up towards the knee. It looked as though they all had lumps on the backs of their legs.

"They feel all right, don't they?" said Ibby. "Not too uncomfortable?"

"They feel fine," said Brendan.

"Then what's the problem?"

The problem was that, since Dave had told him to turn up for the match, Brendan had been expecting to feel like a real footballer, and real footballers don't have safety pins in their shorts, and yellow frills at the tops of their legs, and lumps halfway down. But it was great to be in the team at all, and he nearly forgot about the frills and the lumps and the pins.

He was only a sub, but that still counted. Since he had been told at training that he was in the squad, he had practised saying to himself, "I play for Diplow Rangers Under-Eights."

"This isn't just any old friendly game," Dave told them. "Freddie's Fix-it Shop has donated a new cup for the under-eights, and this is the first match in a knockout tournament. If we win this one, we get to play more games, and maybe win the cup. Not very likely, when we've only just begun, but it's worth trying for."

Mum and Finn and Mary K were over in the playground. Mum had promised to come over and watch if Brendan got a chance to play.

"I don't think I will," he told her. "I'm not nearly as good as the others in the team."

"You never know," said Mum.

"You might be lucky," said Finn. "Some of them might break their legs."

Brendan tried to look as though that would be terrible, but of course he had been thinking just the same thought himself.

"See you later," said Mum. "I hope you do get a chance to play. If we come and watch, I'll do my best to keep Mary K out of the way."

Some mothers and fathers always stayed to watch the training on Wednesdays, but today there were far more grown-ups than usual. Brendan thought some of them must belong to the other team, Gadsmere, but none of them were wearing team colours to show which side they were supporting, so he couldn't be sure. Perhaps he would get yellow scarves for Mum and Finn and Mary K, so that they could support him properly.

Then Dave gave a shout and the six players ran over to him.

"Hey, Benjamin!" Dave shouted.

Brendan looked round, wondering who Benjamin was.

"Come on over," said Dave.

"That's not Benjamin," said Ibby. "That's Brendan."

"Sorry," said Dave. "Brendan. Come on. You're in the squad, aren't you?"

"I didn't know I was playing," said Brendan.

"I don't know if you are or not," said Dave. "Right. We're playing against a very good team today. Gadsmere won their last friendly six–one. And they're big. Look at that centre-forward – he's taller than Ibby. But that doesn't mean we can't win. Now, what's the most important thing to remember in football?"

"Winning the ball?" said Bimal.

"Passing?" said Sasha.

"Shooting?" said Nick.

"The most important thing to remember is that you're part of a team."

"Dad!" said Nathan. "Last week you said—"

"All right, Nathan," said Dave. "I don't want you being heroes, grabbing the ball and trying to do it all on your own. It won't work. Watch where your mates are, and if you're in a good place to receive the ball, call for it. Then look out to see where it should go next. The next most important thing is, keep going. If Gadsmere get a goal in, which they may well do, don't think that's the end of the world. Better to lose one–nil than two–nil. Better to lose ten–one than ten–nil, if it comes to that. Nothing's settled till the final whistle goes, so I don't want to see you dropping your heads and giving up if they do score. Just keep going."

Brendan listened, but it didn't seem to be much to do with him. Perhaps he could be useful just shouting encouragement.

The referee was one of the Gadsmere mothers. She was wearing black shorts and a black T-shirt. She blew her whistle and tossed a coin to see which way the teams would play. Diplow won, and chose to play towards the playground first.

Brendan had seen other people playing football at school, but this was the most real match that he had ever watched. It was exciting. When the first goal was scored, he cheered and jumped in the air. Then he realized that it was Gadsmere who had scored. He kept quiet after that. One–nil to them. Then Nathan scored and made it one–all. Not too bad.

Brendan could see that the Diplow players weren't always doing what Dave had taught them. Once Sasha got the ball, she kept hold of it, hoping that she would be the one to score. Brendan could see that it would have been better to pass. There was Nick standing in a space with no one marking him. Why didn't he shout to Sasha to pass to him?

Then one of the Gadsmere players got the ball off Sasha and made for the goal where Arjun was nervously waiting. Several Diplow players followed alongside, but none of them tried to tackle and get the ball back. Brendan could see that the only hope was to get in and have a go. He felt that if he was on the pitch he would do a better job than any of them.

Suddenly Gadsmere scored again. Two–one. Arjun wasn't a brilliant goalkeeper. Brendan thought he could have jumped and stopped that last one.

The ball went back to the centre, and straight away it was down at Arjun's end again. Arjun was chewing his fingers. Ibby tackled, the Gadsmere player took a shot and missed. Brendan let out a long relieved breath.

Dave called something to the referee, and then he shouted, "Bernard!"

Bernard must be one of the other fathers.

"Hey, Bernard!" he shouted again. "You're on!"

Arjun stopped chewing his fingers and came jogging towards Brendan, peeling off his baggy blue sweatshirt.

"Go on," he said to Brendan.

"What?" said Brendan.

"You're on," said Arjun. "I'm coming off."

Sub

"But he said Bernard," said Brendan, and then remembered that he had been Brian and Bradley and Benjamin before now. "What do I do?"

"Put this on," said Arjun, throwing him the blue sweatshirt. "It's a goal kick."

"Now? Me?" said Brendan.

"Come on, Bernard!" Dave yelled. "Get a move on!"

Brendan ran to the goal, pushing his arms through the sleeves. It didn't seem worth putting on a sweatshirt for just one kick, but perhaps that was the rule. There was the ball. All he had to do was kick it. He should be able to do that all right. He kicked it, and it was a good kick. The ball went three quarters of the way down the pitch. Brendan started to pull the sweatshirt off again.

"What are you doing?" shouted Arjun, who was standing behind the goal. "You can't take it off!"

Brendan turned to look at him. Didn't Arjun want his jumper back? Brendan wandered back to talk to him.

"Where are you going?" said Arjun. "Get back in goal!"

"Am I the goalie now?" said Brendan. "I thought I was just taking the kick."

"You can't do that in a real match," said Arjun. "Once you come on, you stay on."

"But then it's me who has to keep all the goals out," said Brendan, horrified.

He hurried back to the front of the goal. So he really was in the team now. Standing on the sideline it had been easy to see what everyone else was doing wrong. Now he knew that he was worse than any of them, and he hadn't a hope of keeping out any goals. He was the most useless player in the squad. He should have said he had a bad leg and couldn't play.

"Good luck, Brendan!" Ibby shouted. "Come on, Diplow!"

Brendan knew it was no good giving up. Diplow Under-Eights needed their goalkeeper. He must remember everything he had learnt at training. What had Dave said? The most important thing to remember was being part of a team. But here in the goal it was difficult to be part of the team. It was lonely. Brendan wished he was running about with the others instead of waiting here, all by himself, for something terrible to happen.

The ball was still down the other end. That was all right. Ibby had it. Now Sasha. Now Ibby. It would be good if Ibby scored. Brendan hopped from foot to foot. Now he couldn't see the ball. Then almost at once it came whistling past Brendan into the goal. Brendan didn't see where it came from. He had no time to do anything to stop it. Three–one.

He had let in a goal. He wasn't any good as a goalkeeper. He had never thought he would be any good. He was only good at kicking the ball. No good at dribbling, or winning the ball, or shooting, not even any good at running. And no good at all at saving goals. Useless.

"Bad luck, Brendan!" Ibby shouted. "Keep going!"

"Keep going" was what Dave had said. The second most important thing in football. Brendan must keep going and stop any more goals going in. Three–one was better than four–one.

Sasha took the centre, but a Gadsmere boy intercepted the ball and it came horribly close to Brendan's end. Luckily Nick got it away and Brendan could breathe again. He hopped about, ready to spring one way or the other the next time Gadsmere had a shot at goal. He thought it was easiest to jump up, but these under-eights goals weren't very high. It was more likely that he would have to jump left or right.

His chance came almost at once. A Gadsmere player kicked the ball from halfway down the pitch. Brendan watched it coming towards him. This was his chance to make a great save. You couldn't have longer to prepare for a save. He stepped to the right, then decided that more was needed. He threw himself on the ground, arms stretched out towards the ball. Just missed. The ball rolled on just a centimetre beyond his outstretched fingers. But it was outside the goal anyway. The score was still three–one, and Brendan hadn't made any difference.

"Great dive, Brendan!" Ibby shouted.

Brendan felt grateful to Ibby. He had been feeling rather silly, lying on the ground when he needn't have bothered. Ibby was nice. Brendan got to his feet and rubbed his arm.

Whistle. Goal kick. At least that was what he was good at.

"Well played, Aidan," said Dave. Brendan wished that Dave would learn his name.

Then it was four–one. It happened very suddenly. Brendan did try to dive, but diving wasn't the right thing to do. The ball went over his head. Brendan wished that Arjun could come back on instead of him.

The next time, Brendan made a real save. It was an easy one because the ball came so slowly, but if he hadn't scooped it up as it came towards him it would have been a goal. He had made the difference between four–one and five–one. Dave was right. It was worth keeping going.

He kicked the ball as far as he could. It went right down the far end, and suddenly the score was four–two. Sasha had headed the ball into the far goal. Four–two. Not so bad.

Diplow Under-Eights seemed to cheer up. The ball hardly came down Brendan's end at all. He almost wished it would, so that he could try diving for it again. There was a shout. Four–three. He hadn't seen who scored. Perhaps they would win, and he would be on the winning side. He wondered whether Mum and Finn and Mary K were watching, but he didn't dare look for them. He must keep watching the game.

Straight after the centre, the ball came dangerously near, in a tangle of legs. Brendan wanted to go and join in, but he thought he had better not leave the goal. Then someone kicked the ball out towards him. He wasn't sure if he was in the area where he was allowed to pick it up, so he kicked it, and back it went to safety. Sasha kicked it to Nick, but a Gadsmere player got in between them and stood with the ball at his feet, wondering who to pass it to. Ibby dashed up and got the ball away from him, then hit it straight into the goal.

"Lucky we aren't playing the offside rule," said Arjun from behind Brendan.

"It's four–all, isn't it?" said Brendan.

The whistle went for the end of the game. A draw. Brendan remembered that if he hadn't let in that goal, Diplow would have won four–three. But then, if he hadn't saved that other goal, Gadsmere would have won four–three. A draw was all right. Not bad for his first game.

Extra Time

Ibby hadn't expected Brendan to be brought on. He hadn't expected him to play for months, or maybe years. He really was quite a bad footballer. But you could see that he was trying hard, and Ibby ran down to encourage him.

Brendan was saying to Arjun, "That's not bad, is it, four–all?"

"It'll go to extra time," Arjun said.

"Extra time?" said Brendan. He suddenly looked exhausted, and Ibby remembered how a few weeks ago he could hardly run round the pitch. "How long?"

"Maybe ten more minutes," said Ibby. "We can't have a draw when we're playing for a cup, can we? We have to decide which team's going on to the next round. You're doing fine, Brendan. Keep it up!"

"Couldn't Arjun change back in?" Brendan asked.

"I don't think so," said Ibby. "But it won't be your fault if they score. We've all got to stop it getting down here." But he wished they had someone better in goal. He ran back to his position.

The whistle blew. Ibby knew that they couldn't depend on Brendan, so he played even harder than before, fighting to keep the ball away from Brendan's end, even if he couldn't manage to score himself.

When the ball went out, Ibby glanced down at Brendan. He was bouncing about, probably thinking how he would just tip the ball outside the post or over the bar and everyone would cheer. Ibby hoped that he was watching the game.

Then the whistle blew again. Ten minutes was up, and it was still four–all. Brendan was relieved. He hadn't let in any shameful goals.

"It'll probably be golden goal now," Arjun told Brendan.

Brendan waited for him to explain.

"You play until someone scores a goal, and then that's it. That's the winning goal."

"Or the losing goal," said Brendan gloomily. "If Diplow lose, it will be all my fault."

"Hang on," said Ibby, who had been watching Dave talking to the referee. "It might not be golden goal. It might be penalties."

Ibby had felt proud of Brendan when Dave put him in goal. He really hadn't done badly. But in a penalty shoot-out it would all be up to Brendan. Ibby wished that Tariq had given them some goalkeeping practice.

"Penalty shoot-out," Arjun was saying. "Bad luck."

"What is a shoot-out?" said Brendan. It sounded like the sort of film that Mum wouldn't let him watch on television. "How does it work? Do I have to shoot out of the goal, instead of in?"

"You just stop the goals going in," said Arjun. "At least it's all over quickly."

"Don't worry," said Ibby. "Just watch the

ball and do your best."

"Over here, Bertram," Dave shouted. Brendan suspected that Dave was teasing him. He must know his name by now. Rather slowly he joined the rest of the team.

Dave told them what they had to do. Brendan wasn't the only one who didn't know. Three players from each side would take turns to have a shot at goal, with nobody except the goalkeeper to get in the way. The team with the most goals would be the winner. Sasha, Ibby and Nick were Diplow's three.

Ibby put his arm round Brendan's shoulders. "You'll be fine," he said. "I've noticed one thing that could be useful: that big girl with the beads in her hair always goes for the left-hand corner. It was her that made the shot that you dived for, and the one that

Arjun saved, and the first one they scored in the first half. So you can be ready for her at least. Her left, your right."

"What happens?" said Brendan. "I just stand there and they're allowed to kick the ball at me?"

"If they kick it *at* you, you're all right," said Ibby. "But if they kick one way, and you go the other, it's just too bad. Tariq says you can't blame the goalie in a penalty shoot-out, because it's as much luck as skill."

Gadsmere won the toss, so Diplow were the first to shoot. Sasha went first. Ibby watched Gadsmere's goalkeeper. He crouched in the goal, ready to spring. He held his arms out to his sides and looked ready to catch the ball whichever way it went. Ibby wished that Brendan was as much of a goalie.

Sasha took a run up and fired the ball into

the net. The goalie jumped sideways, but too late, and the ball went straight in. The goalie lifted his hands, as though he couldn't have been expected to stop the ball, and got out of the goal. Brendan took his place.

It was the girl with beads in her hair. She looked straight at Brendan and smiled. What did that mean? He watched her eyes. She looked at the left-hand corner of the goal, on Brendan's right, where Ibby had said she would aim for. But then she looked at the right-hand corner as well.

"Remember, Brendan," Ibby called, and Brendan nodded.

The girl went for the ball, and Brendan was already over to that side. Yes! Ibby had been right! The ball was heading straight for Brendan, but hard. Very hard. Brendan would never hold it. Brendan caught it and clutched it to his chest, but it made him stagger backwards. He dropped the ball. There was a cheer. Yes, he'd saved it! No, it was the Gadsmere supporters cheering. He'd dropped the ball inside the line. Gadsmere had scored a goal.

Ibby saw Brendan's chin moving and his eyes opening very wide to stop tears from falling out as he moved away from the goal.

"One each," Ibby called out from where he was lining up to take his penalty. "That's all right. That was nearly a brilliant save."

It was Ibby's turn next. He took a deep breath and puffed it out again through his lips.

"Good luck, Ibby," Brendan remembered to call.

Ibby's shot didn't go in. It wasn't fast enough, and the Gadsmere keeper got to it easily. This was terrible. Ibby knew that Brendan would let the next goal in and they would lose. Brendan would feel that it was all his fault for letting the goal in and would have to be cheered up, but Ibby knew that it was just as much his own fault for not scoring just now, and didn't feel like cheering anyone up.

Luckily the next Gadsmere player was a very small boy. Brendan had noticed that he was fast on the pitch but couldn't kick the ball very hard, and when the shot came it was easy for him to catch. Ibby was relieved to see him stand still after he had caught it, and he didn't put it down until Nick was on the penalty spot waiting for his shot. Then he kicked it to Nick and ran to the side to make way for the Gadsmere keeper.

"Great save, Brendan!" said Ibby.

Nick and the next Gadsmere player both

missed. That was all right. One–all.

"Does that mean it's a draw, after all?" Brendan asked.

"Sudden death," said Ibby.

Brendan looked at him in horror. That sounded even worse than a shoot-out.

"It's like best of one, instead of best of three," Ibby said. "One shot for each side, and, if it's still equal, then another shot for each side, until someone goes ahead."

Nathan went first and scored a brilliant goal. Ibby felt pleased and jealous at the same time. The ball curved round to the right and went in just beside the post. The keeper didn't have a chance. Ibby heard everyone congratulating Nathan, and wished it had been him.

Unluckily the next Gadsmere player also scored a brilliant goal. At least, it was too brilliant for Brendan. It was in the back of the net before he'd started to move.

"Go on, Marcus," said Dave.

Marcus strolled calmly up to the ball with his arms dangling. Suddenly he kicked and scored.

Brendan moved back into the goal.

"Keep going, Brendan!" Ibby shouted to him. If Brendan saved the next goal, then Diplow had won. It didn't look very likely. Ibby decided to hope that one of the Gadsmere players would simply miss.

The next player was a tall thin boy. Not powerful, but maybe clever. Ibby saw Brendan watching him carefully. He glanced at Ibby, but Ibby didn't have any advice for him. The boy dropped his chin onto his chest, as though he was thinking hard. Ibby hoped that Brendan was ready for some quick thinking. All Brendan's thinking would have to be packed into the fraction of a second as the ball came flying past him.

Suddenly the boy kicked the ball, and Brendan sent his left hand to where it was heading. It was the far edge of the goal, and he had to jump to follow his hand, but somehow his legs seemed to know what to do and leapt at just the right time. His left hand stopped the ball, and his right hand came round to clamp it tightly. He fell to the ground and felt his shoulder and thigh crash numb on the grass. But the ball was safe. Ibby was amazed. He ran over to him.

"Fantastic, Brendan! You all right?" He heaved Brendan to his feet.

"I didn't really mean to," said Brendan. "It just happened."

"Of course you meant to," said Ibby,

banging him on the back. "It was just too fast to know what you were meaning. It was brilliant. We've won."

"Well done, Brendan," said Dave. At last he had got the name right.

"Good save, Brendan," said Tariq.

"I didn't know you were going to practise goal-shooting after the match was over," said Mum.

"Mum!" said Brendan. "That *was* the match! It was sudden death, and they suddenly lost, because I saved that goal."

"Really?" said Mum doubtfully.

"Really," said Ibby. "It was a very good save." He sounded surprised, but that was fair. Brendan had been surprised too.

"Bor," said Mary K, clinging round Brendan's tummy.

"We've been teaching her to say 'ball'," said

Finn. "Haven't we taught her well?"

Ibby thought that his own teaching had gone quite well too. He was glad that he'd kept on at Brendan. It wouldn't have to be all kindness from now on. They could just enjoy playing football together.

Ibby hoped he hadn't been too bossy. Football is the best thing in the world, but it may not be the only thing. Perhaps there were other things that Brendan would like them to do together.

Ibby fetched one of the practice balls and rolled it towards Mary K.

"Here, Mary K," he said. "Here's the ball!"

Mary K let go of Brendan. She took no notice of the ball but staggered towards Ibby and threw her arms round him.

Brendan was watching anxiously. Would Ibby think that Mary K was too big to be hugging him, or too dribbly? Perhaps Ibby was only a football friend. It was good to have a football friend, very good. If it hadn't been for Ibby, Brendan wouldn't have been in Diplow Rangers Under-Eights. He wouldn't have saved that goal. But it would be difficult if Ibby wanted him only as a football friend, and the rest of his life had to be kept out of the way.

But Ibby put his arms round Mary K. "Now that you can *say* 'ball'," he said, "we can start teaching you to kick it."

Then Brendan knew that Ibby was a real friend. They could enjoy anything together, even if it was a bit dribbly.